Margaret Hillert's
The Ball Book

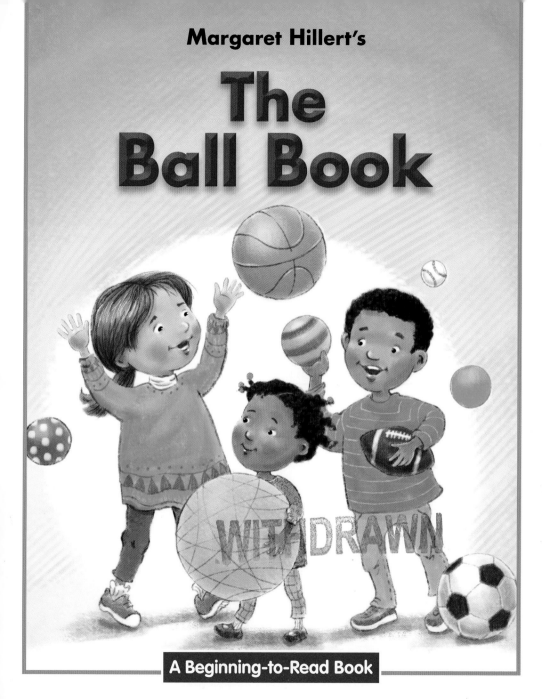

A Beginning-to-Read Book

Illustrated by Paige Billin–Frye

DEAR CAREGIVER,

The books in this Beginning-to-Read collection may look somewhat familiar in that the original versions could have been a part of your own early reading experiences. These carefully written texts feature common sight words to provide your child multiple exposures to the words appearing most frequently in written text. These new versions have been updated and the engaging illustrations are highly appealing to a contemporary audience of young readers.

Begin by reading the story to your child, followed by letting him or her read familiar words and soon your child will be able to read the story independently. At each step of the way, be sure to praise your reader's efforts to build his or her confidence as an independent reader. Discuss the pictures and encourage your child to make connections between the story and his or her own life. At the end of the story, you will find reading activities and a word list that will help your child practice and strengthen beginning reading skills. These activities, along with the comprehension questions are aligned to current standards, so reading efforts at home will directly support the instructional goals in the classroom.

Above all, the most important part of the reading experience is to have fun and enjoy it!

Shannon Cannon

Shannon Cannon,
Literacy Consultant

Norwood House Press • www.norwoodhousepress.com
Beginning-to-Read™ is a registered trademark of Norwood House Press.
Illustration and cover design copyright ©2017 by Norwood House Press. All Rights Reserved.

Authorized adapted reprint from the U.S. English language edition, entitled The Ball Book by Margaret Hillert. Copyright © 2017 Margaret Hillert. Reprinted with permission. All rights reserved. Pearson and The Ball Book are trademarks, in the US and/or other countries, of Pearson Education, Inc. or its affiliates. This publication is protected by copyright, and prior permission to re-use in any way in any format is required by both Norwood House Press and Pearson Education. This book is authorized in the United States for use in schools and public libraries.

Designer: Lindaanne Donohoe
Editorial Production: Lisa Walsh

LIBRARY OF CONGRESS CATALOGING-IN-PUBLICATION DATA
Names: Hillert, Margaret, author. I Billin-Frye, Paige, illustrator.
Title: The ball book / by Margaret Hillert ; illustrated by Paige Billin-Frye.
Description: Chicago, IL : Norwood House Press, 2016. I Series: A beginning-to-read book I Summary: People play a variety of games involving balls on the big ball that is Earth. Includes reading activities and a word list. I Description based on print version record and CIP data provided by publisher; resource not viewed.
Identifiers: LCCN 2016020719 (print) I LCCN 2016001840 (ebook) I ISBN 9781603579568 (eBook) I ISBN 9781599537948 (library edition : alk. paper)
Subjects: I CYAC: Ball games--Fiction. I Balls (Sporting goods)--Fiction. I Games--Fiction.
Classification: LCC PZ7.H558 (print) I LCC PZ7.H558 Bal 2016 (ebook) I DDC [E]--dc23
LC record available at https://lccn.loc.gov/2016020719

288N—072016
Manufactured in the United States of America in North Mankato, Minnesota.

Balls, balls, balls.
Big balls. Little balls.
Balls for you and me.

I like balls.
I can play with this one.
I make it go up and down.

You can play with me.
Look out.
Here it comes.
Get it. Get it.

This is fun to play.
The ball is a little one.
Can you get this little ball?

Look at the little ones here.
Pretty little ones.
Make one go in.
Make one go out.

Here is a big ball.
You can jump on it.
Jump, jump, jump.

And here is one for the cat.
Something is in this little ball.
The cat will run and get it.

This is a little ball, too.
I make it go.

You make it go.
We have fun with it.

You have to get this ball up.
Up, up, and in.
You have to work at it.
Work, work, work.

Now look at this ball.
You can make something go
down with it.
Down, down, down.

Good, good.
You did it!

You did it!
Good for you.

And this is fun, too.

You have to run, run, run
to get this ball.
Oh, my. Oh, my.

Father and Mother like to play with this ball.

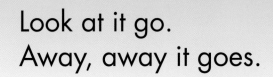

Look at it go.
Away, away it goes.

Look up, up, up.

Get this ball up.
Help it go.

This is good to play at school.
But you have to look out!
Look out for this ball.

Here is a funny ball.
Can you guess what it is for?
What can you do with it?

This is what you
do with it.
You run and run
and run.

We can play with this ball,
and we see it on TV.
We run and run with
this ball, too.

This ball is fun to play with.
You are good at this.
Mother and Father come to
see you play.

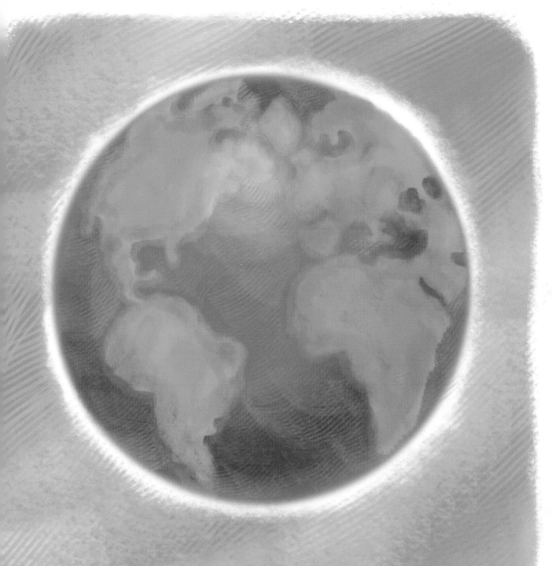

This is a big, big, BIG ball!
We are on this ball.
That is funny.

We work on it.
We play on it.

What a good ball it is!

Foundational Skills

In addition to reading the numerous high-frequency words in the text, this book also supports the development of foundational skills.

Phonological Awareness: The Phonograms –all and -ook

Oral Blending: Say the beginning and ending parts of the following words and ask your child to listen to the sounds and say the whole word:

/b/ + all = ball	/f/ + all = fall	/t/ + all = tall	/w/ + all = wall
/m/ + all = mall	/h/ + all = hall	/b/ + ook = book	/l/ + ook = look
/c/ + ook = cook	/t/ + ook = took	/h/ + ook = hook	/n/ + ook = nook

Phonics: The letters b, c, f, h, l, m, n, t

1. Fold a piece of paper in half down the middle. Draw a line on the fold.
2. At the top of the paper, to the left of the line, write the phonogram __**all**.
3. At the top of the paper, to the right of the line, write the phonogram __**ook**.
4. Write the letters **b, c, f, h, l, m, n, t** on small pieces of paper.
5. Using the letters, ask your child to make as many **–all** and **–ook** words as he or she can and to write those words in the correct column.

Fluency: Shared Reading

1. Reread the story to your child at least two more times while your child tracks the print by running a finger under the words as they are read. Ask your child to read the words he or she knows with you.
2. Reread the story taking turns, alternating readers between sentences or pages.

Language

The concepts, illustrations, and text in this book help children develop language both explicitly and implicitly.

Vocabulary: Adjectives

1. Explain to your child that words that describe something are called adjectives.

2. Say the following adjectives and ask your child to name something that the adjective might describe:

cold	pretty	huge	fast	hot	scratchy
soft	loud	tiny	slow	funny	delicious

3. Explain to your child that adjectives can sometimes describe a type of something. The story is about many different kinds of balls.

4. Ask your child to name the different kinds of balls in the story. Write the words that describe the kinds of balls in the story on sticky note paper.

5. Mix the words up and randomly say each word to your child. Ask your child to point to the correct word.

6. Ask your child to place the sticky notes on the pages in the book where the adjective describes the kind of ball on that page.

Reading Literature and Informational Text

To support comprehension, ask your child the following questions. The answers either come directly from the text or require inferences and discussion.

Key Ideas and Detail

- Ask your child to retell the sequence of events in the story.
- How many different balls were used in this book?

Craft and Structure

- Is this a book that tells a story or one that gives information? How do you know?
- How do you think the people in the story feel when they are playing games?

Integration of Knowledge and Ideas

- What kinds of ball games can you play alone?
- Why do you think the author says we live on a ball?

WORD LIST

The Ball Book uses the 62 words listed below.

This list can be used to practice reading the words that appear in the text. You may wish to write the words on index cards and use them to help your child build automatic word recognition. Regular practice with these words will enhance your child's fluency in reading connected text.

a	Father	I	oh	that
and	for	in	on	the
are	fun	is	one(s)	this
at	funny	it	out	to
away				too
	get	jump	play	TV
ball(s)	go		pretty	
big	goes	like		up
but	good	little	run	
	guess	look		we
can			school	what
cat	have	make	see	will
come(s)	help	me	something	with
	here	Mother		work
did		my		
do				you
down		now		

ABOUT THE AUTHOR Margaret Hillert has helped millions of children all over the world learn to read independently. She was a first grade teacher for 34 years and during that time started writing books that her students could both gain confidence in reading and enjoy. She wrote well over 100 books for children just learning to read. As a child, she enjoyed writing poetry and continued her poetic writings as an adult for both children and adults.

Photograph by Glenna Washburn

ABOUT THE ILLUSTRATOR Paige Billin–Frye studied illustration and design at Washington University in St. Louis. Before she began illustrating for children she designed department store ads, illustrated posters and magazine covers, and painted greeting cards. She has served as president and treasurer of The Children's Book Guild. She has also been honored by having her illustrations included in The Original Art show at The Society of Illustrators in New York. www.paigebillinfrye.com